The Uncovered Policeman

The first story in the Rags to Riches series

By Ted Bun

February 2016

ISBN-10: 1537490672

ISBN-13: 978-1537490670

This is a story is a complete fiction.

The characters are not intended to reflect any living person. If you think you might be one of the characters in the story, please get in touch. You sound like a nice person.

I must apologise for any technical errors:
    I have no experience of Police work.
    I have no experience of solicitors, beyond being robbed by them during a divorce.
    I am a naturist so that bit should be close to being correct.

So please forgive me my mistakes this time, I will try not to make them again.

I hope you enjoy the story...
Ted

Contents

Burglary in a Naturist Resort

"Charlie 1 5, Charlie 1 5."

nobody in particular, as he lifted the radio mike off the dash in his patrol car. Addy was nearing the end of his second year in the police force.

It was a job he had taken after deciding that seasickness made his life in the Navy impossible. He had enjoyed the service life. The Training Ship and his shore-based posting at Portsmouth had been great fun. His second posting to a small fisheries protection vessel had been much less so. He was seasick, horribly and continually seasick. Every time the sea got rougher than dead flat calm, Addy was hanging over the side of the ship-saying goodbye to everything he had ever eaten. In fact, after six months he had asked to be transferred on medical grounds. Once off the ship, he discovered he was going to be made redundant, 'Defence Cuts'.

Out of the Navy, with no pension and no plan for the future. He had not been expecting to leave the Navy for another ten years; he did not know what to do next. Living on his dwindling redundancy money, he was aimless and bored. Addy had enjoyed the

6

disciplined life in the Navy and found Civvy Street without a job an uncomfortable place.

One evening, heading home from the pub slightly the worse for wear, he was stopped and spoken to by a Police Constable. The PC suggested to Addy that singing about his time as 'a wild rover', at the top of his voice, on a residential street, at half-past midnight (where had the evening gone??) was not in the public interest. That it might be best for all if Addy was to tiptoe off home before singing the second verse when a Police Sergeant walked up. He took the PC to one side and requested the PC wrapped up dealing with the D and D (drunk and disorderly). He had a more important job that he wanted him to help with.

"Yes, Sarg, right away, Sarg." Turning to Addy, "Ok you. Home. Quietly. Now!"

Next morning, as he sipped a strong black coffee in the kitchen of his small flat, Addy reflected on the conversation. Not what had been said to him so much as what passed between the Sargent and the Constable. The Constable was about his age, he had a responsible job, a smart uniform and was part of an organised team. He reminded Addy of Seaman Adiscombe RN in many ways. There it was. The discipline and structure he was looking for. This was going to be his new career. He was going to become a policeman! Thanking goodness that he hadn't been arrested last night. He went to the library to look up how to apply to the police force.

That was three eventful years ago. He had been through the application process, the Assessment Centre and the Fitness Test. He had worked through the college courses and had impressed during his probation period. That was now behind him and promotion, or maybe a move to CID, ahead if he worked hard and followed the rules.

"1 5, receiving. What is your message? Over."

"1 5, we have a report of a burglary on licensed premises, can you attend?"

"1 5, mark me as attending. What is the address?"

"1 5, you are going to love this," replied the dispatcher, breaking RT protocol. "The Club House at Eden Gardens Naturist Resort."

"This will be fun… NOT!" Addy thought to himself. "I can see the stick I am going to get from the lads over this one."

"1 5, Attending." He sighed.

Eden Gardens

Eden Gardens Naturist Resort is situated on the outskirts of the urban sprawl of the once compact market town. On three sides, the houses were now very close to the fence that had been put up to screen the Resort from prying eyes.

Back in the 1950s, when it had opened as Eden Gardens Sun Club, it had been on four acres of largely barren wilderness surrounded by farmland. The enterprising Brigadier Weston – Hyde had retired after a career in the army that had seen him through the war and safely into peacetime. In his various postings during the war years, he had served in many places, mainly in the Pacific, where he had been in charge of the Air Defence of what is now Samoa. Where he had enjoyed the freedom of swimming and sunbathing naked on the tropical beaches. On returning to the UK, he had been involved in the decommissioning of temporary headquarters and Special Services buildings that had been taken over by the War Department. Most of them were returned, in a very battered state, to their owners with hardly a word of thanks.

Measham Hall was not as lucky as some, it was in very poor condition, having been the temporary home for four different regiments from three different continents in the months leading up to D-Day. The family that had been the owners had been all but destroyed by the War. The father had been killed in the battle at Calais, defending the Dunkirk evacuation. His son was shot down and presumed killed over Hamburg in 1943; his daughter was caught in a blast from a V2 in the dying days of the war in Europe. The Mother of the family, distraught at her losses and burdened with death duties was unable to cope with the restoration of the Hall. When the damp and aged wiring finally gave up the ghost and the fire started, it was the end.

When his services were no longer required by Her Majesty, the Brigadier took his gratuity, pension and a small inheritance from his family and went in search of something new. He wasn't sure what, but there had to be something.

Waiting for the train at Marylebone Station, he chose to idle away a few minutes looking at an estate agent's advertisement, when a description of a derelict country house caught his eye. It was a place he had helped decommission. Beautiful surroundings, as he recalled. Later that afternoon he was back wandering around what remained of Measham Hall.

11

The House was gone, most of the land had been rented out, but the gardens and some of the outbuildings remained.

As he wandered around, he could see that the old chauffeur's cottage was repairable and the gardens, the lawns and the formal orchards could be restored. The day was warm and as he meandered he had removed his tie and jacket, then, he had unbuttoned his shirt. As he came around the corner, into what had once been a walled garden, he discovered the disused swimming pool. The pool, along with what he had already seen, started to crystallise an idea in his mind. He sat down on his jacket and thought.

It got warmer ... soon he was getting uncomfortable, so he removed the rest of his heavy woollen clothes and sat naked in the sun trying to make the sums work.

Slowly, he did the calculations in his mind, he could afford to buy the place and his pension would cover the costs of the refurbishment of the cottage and still have enough left to live on, frugally, but enough. It was getting the grounds restored and the pool sorted out that would need more money and more help. Not a lot, but still more than he alone could afford. As the sun dropped below the trees, he dressed and started to walk back towards the station. On his way there, he passed a copse and a sudden noise made him look over the hedgerow.

What he saw filled in the missing pieces for him.

He watched as four youngsters scrambled for their towels, or the safety of their tent, as an angry farmer stormed across the field demanding they vacate his land immediately. The four young people were as naked as he himself had been just a few minutes earlier.

All he now needed was to convince his wife.

Six months later, in April 1955, the first Eden Gardens Sun Club members working party started clearing the old walled garden.

A Policeman Investigates

The Eden Gardens Naturist Resort that Addy drove up to had changed considerably from the old Sun Club. The members club had gone, replaced by a modern holiday park. Chalets and mobile homes had replaced the tents and the grounds were groomed.

Having been 'buzzed' through the gate, Addy drove slowly past a row of neat chalets towards the clubhouse. A man, dressed in a T-Shirt and a pair of shorts, stood outside the door. As Addy got out of the car, the man called out for him to come around to the right of the building. Pointing to an open door with a smashed pane of glass.

"I think they got in through here," he began.

Addy looked around and thought, "Well ten out of ten for observation," but keeping his professional manner, he started, "I'm PC Adiscombe, can I have your name, sir?"

"Sean Cutter, I am the resort owner, along with my wife and of course the bank!" He added with a wry grin.

Gradually he drew all the information out of Sean. He had locked up at 10:30 pm the previous evening. As it was a Sunday, most of the day visitors had left, "What with work and school today." There were about a half dozen of the mobile homes occupied by guests, but these people often stayed in after sunset, eating and sharing a bottle of wine or a few beers, rather than going to the bar. It had gone quiet, so he closed up and went home, watched a bit of TV with his wife and then they had gone to bed.

In the morning, he had come over to air the building and restock the bar and found glass all over the place.

Addy called in and asked for a Scene of Crime Officer (SOCO) to come and do forensics. With a few cases of Scotch and other spirits, along with several hundred pounds in cash, this crime had crossed the threshold for a full investigation.

While he waited for the SOCO to arrive, his radio having remained remarkably silent, Addy decided to take a look around to see if there were any signs of intruders entering the grounds. Starting at a point about fifty yards from the clubhouse he started to walk in a clockwise circle around it looking for anything that might show how the criminals had either approached or escaped from, the scene of the crime.

As he walked, studying the ground, he noticed how peaceful it was in the resort. There was a stand of trees a further twenty-five or so yards beyond where he was walking, he assumed that marked the fence line.

"I'll wander over there and take a look at the fence in that area later," he noted mentally.

Continuing around to the next side of the building, he found an open expanse of carefully maintained lawn that sloped gently down to a swimming pool protected by a low wire fence and what looked to be tennis courts with much higher wire fences off to one side.

"Wow! It must be nice here on a warm summer's day," he thought to himself, as the professional in him noted that escape that way was unlikely, because of all the fences.

At what he had classified as the front of the building, there was a terrace along this south-facing aspect, with what looked like a large barbeque built into the wall at the far end. Two hundred or maybe

16

two hundred and fifty yards away across the lawn were a row of mobile homes where he could see a few parked cars, indicating that there were other people around. In front of him was the roadway he had driven in along, with the row of chalets that ended near the Club House to allow for the car park, where he could see the SOCO getting her gear out of the car. He noted that Sean and a woman in a loose dress were talking with the SOCO. Addy picked up the pace and went over to join them.

"Hello, I'm PC Adiscombe," he introduced himself to the SOCO, and by default to the woman.

"Jane Deene," replied the civilian scientist, "I was just explaining to Mr and Mrs Cutter here that I will try to get some fingerprints and have a look around for any blood or other bodily fluids for DNA, but not to get their hopes too high, as it is a public space," she paused. "Well, sort of … lots of people legally being here!"

To help Jane out from the hole she appeared to be digging herself into, Addy turned to Mrs Cutter, "Do you live on-site, Mrs Cutter?" he enquired.

"Why? Yes," she replied, turning to face Addy.

"Did you hear or see anything unusual last night?" He enquired.

"No, I don't think so," she replied.

"I will still need a statement from you and Mr Cutter. Is there somewhere we can sit while I do this?"

"Could we do it in an hour or so? I have to take my mother to the doctor for a blood test in a few minutes." Mrs Cutter explained. "She lives in town, so you won't need to take a statement from her too," she smiled.

"I have to go and do the pool about now as well," explained Sean. "The insurance like to see it being done nice and regular in case someone gets ill soon after using it, I dunno bleedin' 'elf and safety," he finished with a smile.

"That's fine, I need to see if anyone else heard or saw anything last night. Shall we meet inside? I imagine Jane will have finished making her mess by then?"

"Yes, PC Adiscombe," came the frosty response from the SOCO, "I should have finished dusting for prints by then."

"OK, I'll go and make enquiries at the places over there," he pointed to the mobile homes. "Oh! And later I'll want to look at the fence behind that stand of

18

trees," he nodded towards where he felt the intruders might have gained access.

"You..." began Jane.

"You'll have a long walk then," Sean announced across her, "Our house is behind those trees and then there is the camping ground."

"Ah, in that case, I'll need to take a proper look around; I thought I could see most of the place from here. I'll see you both in about, say an hour and a half?"

Addy walked off back towards the road he had driven in along, in the direction of the mobile homes, where he had seen the cars.

"Thanks for covering that one up for me Sean, I nearly slipped up there."

"You know we always have our members' interests at heart, Jane," he replied. "Gill went and warned most of the guests we had an Officer of the Law around. Meanwhile, you know your way around and I've still got that pool to do,"

☐

The Eyes have it

It had been over half an hour since he had arrived at Eden Gardens and the day was starting to warm up nicely. Addy first walked to his patrol car and removed his tunic jacket. He had seen the weather forecast last night and, for the first time, he had put on his short-sleeved summer uniform shirt that morning. It was after all late May.

As he strode along the road towards the mobile homes, he heard a door slam off to his right.

'I didn't notice any cars on this side,' he thought as he scanned the line of chalets for the source of the noise.

It didn't take him long to spot it.

Emerging from the next chalet in the row was a young woman, probably mid-twenties he guessed, about medium height and build with dark brown bobbed hair. She was clutching an arm full of books and a cup of coffee.

20

That he had taken all this in, in a single glance, was remarkable. As he had simultaneously taken the fact that she was completely naked.

"Good morning, Miss!"

'Miss? I never call anyone Miss! She could be married! A radical feminist! And I have just insulted her! I should have said Mizz, or Mam', Oh God!' The thoughts raced through Addy's panic-stricken mind.

"There has been a spot of trouble at the clubhouse." Professional, act professional, "I am making a few enquiries, I'd like to come back and ask you a few questions when … Professional, you're a professional. Man up! "… when you have … got yourself sorted out." Phew!!

Addy walked on trying to regain control over his racing mind and heart.

As he walked away, he did not see the lingering look that followed him up the road until a book slipped, was grabbed at and caught. With a start, Bea came back to life and walked down the steps and over to the table set up in the sunny corner of the front garden of the chalet. Putting down her books, she stood, sipping her coffee, watching Addy as he walked on, along the road.

"Now that is one very fit policeman." She thought to herself. "Nice hairy arms and a fantastic smile. Boy, was he embarrassed!"

She sat down, found her notepad, pulled out her pen and opened her book.

"Contract Law … I hate Contract Law but needs must" she muttered as she started to read and take notes.

It took Addy nearly an hour to speak to the people staying in the mobile homes. Strangely they were all dressed, well sort of. Most of the men wore shorts and T-shirts. Most of the women sported dresses. A few of both sexes wore a wrap of some sort. What was obvious from the way their bodies moved one way as their owners move another way was very few were wearing anything else.

What was also apparent, was that they had seen or heard even less, of any significance, than they were wearing. Which, as he would describe it, was next to nothing

He was walking back towards the clubhouse to check with the SOCO before moving on to complete his exploration of the grounds when a string of curses interrupted his reverie. Ah yes, the nice-looking young lady! He still had to talk to her. Hopefully, by now she will have sorted out some clothes. It would be sad if she had mind you. He had an impression she had a very nice-looking body but it would be so much easier to ask questions of her if she was dressed.

"Ah, there she is," he thought "sat behind that pile of books, of course, she will have one of those wrap thingies or something. Ha! I can see the corner of a towel below the chair." He noted before he knocked on the gate post. Bea looked up and saw Addy standing uncertainly at the gate.

"Come in and talk to me, take me away from these damn books for a few minutes"

"Thank you." Addy stepped into the garden as Bea half rose to meet him, revealing the fact she was still dressed as she had been at their first meeting,

'That impression was right,' he thought 'and those beautiful eyes.'

Bea taking advantage of Addy's momentary loss of equilibrium took control of the conversation "Take a seat, I'll get you a coffee. You look like you need one" She stood up, pointed Addy at a chair and went inside. She was smiling to herself.

"He is nice looking, and I like the way he holds himself straight and tall." She thought to herself as the

23

kettle boiled and she put on a red and white printed wrap. She made a cup of coffee, white and 2 sugars "Well it might help him with the shock." And still smiling at her joke carried it outside.

Addy was starting to recover when he heard her crash through the door. He looked around and watched as she came down the steps "Damn! No! Oh good! She has put something on, those eyes are heavenly and that smile…"

"One coffee NATO Standard" The words crashed into Addy's dream state.

"How did you know how I take my coffee?" Well, that was a question and was here to ask questions and that smile; the way it was dancing in time with her eyes.

"I have a brother and a cousin in the Army, they both now drink it that way and call it NATO Standard, you seem to hold yourself in the same way. I guessed that you have been in the services"

Addy missed every word but had decided that brown was the best colour for eyes. Chocolate brown with flecks of gold, that danced, in time with a smile on the same face.

He sipped his cup of nectar and the taste of coffee brought him back to the here and now.

He hated sweet coffee almost as much as he hated white coffee. This was the best coffee ever.

"I gather that you were getting frustrated with your books," he commented. "I heard some very choice utterances just now"

"Yes, exam revision. That is why I am staying here, to get away from distractions, but right now I need one! Otherwise, I am going to scream"

"What are you studying? Asked Addy. Still unable to focus on business.

"Law, and today it is Contract Law, I hate Contract Law, too much precedent, not enough law!"

Addy took another sip of his coffee and watched the eyes dance. He made a decision, one he hoped was going to change his life for the better.

"I have to look around the grounds here," he announced truthfully "but I don't know the place, would you like to walk with me and make sure I don't get lost?" He continued hopefully.

"I thought there were some questions you wanted to ask me?" Bea reminded him, a smile flashing across her lips as she thought of the fun she could have on this walk.

"We don't have to walk in silence," came the response from an emboldened Addy. 'I would go back to sea for that smile!' he thought to himself.

A few minutes later the police officer in his summer uniform and the scantily dressed naturist were walking past the stand of trees. Past the cottage that was once home to the family chauffeur, then to Brigadier and Mrs Weston-Hyde and was now home to the Cutters. Then on passed the site of the old pool that was now the utility block for the camping area.

An hour later Addy had added a huge number of facts to his investigation. Well no, he hadn't but he had found out a lot about Bea.

As they walked, she told him about being in Eden Gardens studying because the home was crazy. Her little sister was on study leave ahead of her A'levels and was very stressed. Her younger brother was down from university revising for finals and exceedingly stressed. So she had moved out to Grandma's summer place, as the family called it, to study for her Legal Practice Course, the LPC, and get ready for the final stage of training before becoming a solicitor.

He had also learnt that Bea's family had been members at Eden since it opened in 1955 and when her grandfather retired he and his wife had used his lump sum to buy the chalet for the benefit of the whole family. Grandpa had died in 1979 but Grandma had kept the place and the generations had continued to use Grandma's Summer Place as a bolt-hole out of town.

As they walked and talked Bea had become frustrated with having to keep adjusting her wrap and finally untied it and held it in her hand as they walked. Addy hadn't noticed it happening. When he did he realised he had been walking with and talking to a beautiful, intelligent, naked woman and that was fine. He was happy.

He had learnt that there was no way anyone had come over the fence beyond the camping area. The ground was still wet from winter and there was no sign of footprints.

Slightly later than he had said Addy arrived back at the clubhouse. The place was a mess not only the broken glass from the door and the trashing that comes with a careless search but the overlying film of fingerprint powder.

"Ms Deene said she had a few prints that may be useful but nothing else" reported Sean "Do you mind if I start the clear-up while you chat to Gill?"

While Addy recorded Gill Cutter's statement; she went home at about 10:00, watched TV, Sean came in, went to bed and nothing else until Sean came back after phoning the police.

Nothing exciting, routine police work eliminating possibilities.

Sean started opening the clubhouse, He went outside and opened the big shutters along the South wall allowing the light to stream in.

Addy could see he was in a large room with a bar and a small stage and several doors off. Along the south wall were large glass sliding doors out onto the patio.

" I imagine that is popular on a hot summer's day" Addy commented as Sean sat down for his statement.

"Yeah, and in winter when the sun shines in it warms the room up too. Solar heating if you will."

28

"I'd like to look around just in case we have missed anything"

"Feel free, I'll get us both a cuppa"

Addy walked over to the big windows; the aspect was as he thought. The door to the right behind the barbeque led into a well-equipped kitchen. Having a kitchen next to the barbeque made sense. The doors to the left and right of the bar were to the toilets, his and hers. There was the door they had come in through with a corridor full of notice boards and bookshelves full of books and magazines. The last door opened into a large changing room, like the one at the rugby club, with showers and lockers and a door out to the pool and lawns beyond. He looked for the "Away team" dressing room not finding it he realised that both teams used the one dressing room to change into their almost identical strips

After giving his statement, Sean asked "So what is the process from here, Officer?".

Addy explained that he would file all the statements and CID might be in touch and that Sean should ring the station in the morning for a crime number, and pass that on to his insurance company.

As he walked back to his car Addy remembered that he still did not have a statement from Bea.

"Any excuse," he thought and started to walk toward Grandma's summer place.

Bea was back at her books enjoying Contract Law. After all, if it is all precedent … that was where the money was to be made. She looked up as Addy came to the gate.

Suddenly "Charlie 1 5, Charlie 1 5" Addy's radio burst to life.

Addy smiled at Bea and turned to walk away "Charlie 1 5 receiving over"

A few minutes later Addy was back "I have another call. Can I come back later for your statement?"

"Of course, I'm not going anywhere and another break from this stuff later will do me good" and the dancing smile flashed at Addy once more.

Addy was on cloud 9 as he worked his way through the rest of his shift. The call was for a 'domestic'. Then he had to deal with a couple of shoplifting cases. Back at the 'nick', there was a pile of paperwork to complete and suddenly his shift was over. What should he do? He still hadn't taken Bea's statement.

"OK, I'm going to do it on my way home" he announced to himself.

☐

The First Clue

Twenty minutes later he was buzzed in by a slightly bemused Sean.

Bea was slightly disappointed that PC Adiscombe hadn't come back. He was rather nice-looking, he was in good shape and wonderfully shy around her. Was it the accidental loss of her wrap? Was it the teasing? Or was he just a nice guy?

Then there was a knock at the door, she reached for a wrap and thought, "Why? There are only naturists out there."

Just how wrong can a girl get? There was a uniformed policeman ... again! That was twice in one day she had opened the door and found this uniformed policeman outside her place. This time, it was Bea who felt a little embarrassed about her nudity, but then his eyes were fixed on hers not on her breasts, nor anywhere else below her chin. She liked that about him too.

"Sorry about the delay. The day got in the way," were his first words, "but I wanted to get the formalities out of the way." Out of the way of what? The thought passed through both of their minds simultaneously.

Inviting Addy to take a seat on the sofa, Bea took a seat on her towel-covered armchair. The best bit of the statement taking for Addy was the discovery that Beatrice Johnston lived and worked in the same town. That she was single. That she normally lived with her parents and that she was never, ever, Beatrice nor for that matter BJ! Addy could relate to the name thing.

The important thing he learnt was that Bea had heard a bit of noise and clattering around in the bin area behind her chalet at about half past midnight, but thought it was just cats. To help him understand 'the where and the what' that were involved Addy needed to see the scene. Together, the woman, only wrapped in a flimsy sarong, and the police officer walked around to the area where the bins were stored.

There was nothing to be seen in the fading light except the bins arranged against the fence, waiting to be emptied.

"Against the fence," thought the professional "It could be the escape route. I'll need to come back in the daylight to have a look."

"Yes!!! Result!" screamed the mind of a young man who was already totally hooked on Bea.

Addy walked Bea back to her door and at the doorstep, Bea turned to face him.

"I'd offer you a drink, but I suppose it is out of the question with you being on duty?"

"As it happens," he grinned, "I am off duty and have been for about an hour. A drink would be fantastic."

They sat, sipping a glass of wine and talked for hours and parted, promising to meet again tomorrow, whenever Addy could get over, to investigate the bin area in daylight. This time, he had her number so that he could call first.

Next morning at Parade, there were a few comments about how was he getting on with the bare skins, was he able to work out which one was his baton? and other old jokes. He countered by complaining that someone had gone around and warned the naturists he was on site and they all had got dressed. He did admit that one of the fifty-year-old ladies must have been a cracker in her day. His boring, but generally honest, answers eventually dampened the speculation.

Addy was told that CID had no resources for investigating the break-in, but he was going to be allowed a few hours to make a good showing of doing it, in fact, he was ordered to make sure it was a very good showing.

The local paper was always ready to run a story that gave them a chance to be critical of the police. This had started when the Editor's wife was found guilty of driving while over the limit. The story told in the station was that it took a while for the Editor and his wife to get out of the car. Apparently, they had climbed across the seats to get out on the opposite sides of the car from where they had been sitting while the car was in motion. The newspaperman, who, the car crew was convinced had been the driver, could hardly stand up! A story as sexy as the police's failure to look into crime at the naturist resort would be like manna from heaven to the vengeful Editor.

"Oh God, now it is political!" the PC quaked in his boots, "I better get this right, but on the other hand if I do, it could be a door opener for me."

An hour later, Bea met Addy at the gate as he drove up to Eden Gardens. Bea climbed into the police car and they drove to the bin area.

Addy took off his jacket, to allow him to slip on a paper coverall and plastic gloves. He climbed onto one of the bins and looked over the fence, there were clear footprints indicating that two or more people had climbed the fence at this point. Moving down the fence a little way he shinned over and walked back to the crossing point and scouted around. There were two distinct sets of prints. One with a Nike sole and the other looking like a worn Doc Martin boot print. Both came across the field from the Country View Estate. These were not street punks. The Country View was one of the most prestigious estates in town. "Damn, the Assistant Super lives over there somewhere. Make that Political with a capital P!" he thought to himself.

A little distance away from the fence, he saw a pallet that could have been used as a scaling ladder. He pulled his phone out of his pocket and took pictures of the footprints and the pallet. Mind you, connecting this evidence to a suspect was not going to be easy. Still, he would record it. He would do a good job. He would get that CID job!!

He scrambled back over the fence with help from Bea.

"I suppose I should check the bins too. Can you hold my camera please Bea?" He reached into his pocket and held out his rather tatty old-school phone towards Bea. Suddenly it fell, neither of them was concentrating. As the phone had clattered to the ground, it had wound up under a bin but was quickly recovered.

With the phone firmly in Bea's hands, Addy opened the first bin. In the third bin, the one the criminals would have climbed on to exit the Resort, Addy found the Scotch and the other spirits, all three dozen bottles. He assumed they'd had been hidden for later recovery, being too heavy to carry away across the fields. In the fourth bin, he wasn't sure what he found but it was very wet and very smelly and it was through his paper suit and shirt in no time.

Bea held her nose and her eyes dance to the rhythm of her laughter as she dragged Addy back to her chalet so that he could get himself cleaned up. With his paper suit in a black bag and his shirt in the machine on the quick wash and dry cycle he sat with Bea and discussed what to do next.

Bea sat opposite the topless police officer and thought how lucky she was. She could not help herself smiling as his muscles rippled as he moved this way and that to illustrate a point.

The topless policeman found himself captivated alternatively by the dancing eyes and the flickering smile. That they were both associated with an attractive young woman, who happened to be naked, had everything to do with it.

Addy took the plan he and Bea had developed back to the station. Both his Sargent, and later the Inspector, gave him permission to have a few hours of overtime that evening and on Wednesday and Thursday evenings. His mission; to wait for and apprehend the thieves if they came back for the stash before the bins were emptied on Friday.

"Brilliant," thought Addy "I hope they come Thursday. That will give me almost the whole week at Eden Gardens with Bea." In that moment, he realised he was hooked good and proper on the naked lawyer with the dancing eyes.

The Cutter's Tale

Sean listened carefully to the phone as Addy explained his plan to try to catch the thieves. He agreed to help the police.

"Well as you will be here, come into the clubhouse for a meal tonight, we have a social on and the kitchen will be open." Sean had thought it would be nice to have a local police officer on-side with the resort, and Addy seemed to fit the bill.

He and Gill had returned from Spain nearly ten years ago, full of concern for Gill's mother and with the money from the lottery win in their pockets. How different it had been when they had left home to work their way around Europe as volunteer workers.

They had been respected members of the local community running the village store and post office in the area where they had both grown up. They had never made huge amounts but it had been enough for them to live moderately well. Then they got the bad news, the recently reorganised Post Office Limited was going to close their Sub Post Office. The loss of the salary and the impulse purchases by people who came in to use the Post Office services would mean the store would no longer be viable.

Unlike many others who planned to struggle on; Sean decided to follow the advice his father had drummed into him, "Always pay the bank first, if you pay them they will look after you, but your tailor won't."

Instead of borrowing to try to bridge an unbridgeable gap, they sold up to the Pharmacist next door. He got a great deal; they had money in the bank and a happy bank manager.

They had registered with the new Workaway website and had a list of places that were prepared to offer food and a place to sleep in exchange for a few hours of work each day. By working like this, they would be able to eke out the little money they had saved for several years.

Together they had travelled back and forth across Europe, volunteering when paid work was not available. In this way, they managed to stretch their money far longer than they had thought possible and acquired a great many skills. Then after two years, they arrived as volunteers at a campsite on the Spanish Mediterranean coast. The owner's wife had fallen and broken her hip. The owner, Sr. Hernandez, needed help long-term. After they had worked for him for three weeks, he asked if they would stay for the season. He would pay them a few euros each week and they could keep any money they picked up from offering massages, cooking meals or doing repairs.

The site was busy from early in the season. They soon discovered the site was popular with naturists because it was close to, but much less expensive than the Playa Vera Naturist Resort and the naturist beach.

Throughout the summer, they found that the naturists were, on the whole, easier guests to accommodate than the non-naturists, whom they soon came to speak of as textiles.

As the summer drew to a close, Sra. Hernandez was not getting better. She had a raging infection that was not responding well to antibiotics. Sr. Hernandez asked if they would stay in the house over winter while he went with his wife to Madrid for treatment.

They agreed to stay, on the proviso that they could make some changes to the way the site ran for the next summer. The site would become clothing optional; open to people who wanted to be undressed all the time as well as those who preferred to wear clothes. Sean was going to build a bar alongside the existing pool house, close to the pool. They were going to put showers on the wall at the other end of the pool house so people could rinse off the sand and dust before going into the water. Finally, to help keep the water clean, baggy shorts and swimming dresses would be banned from the pool.

The desperate Sr. Hernandez agreed. He didn't understand the naturists, but they filled his campsite all summer long so why not cater for them?

They changed the website and wrote to the various agencies that booked people to announce the clothing-optional policy. Sean built a wooden lean-to hut, which had a hinged half-wall so it could be opened up to give shade from the sun as well as providing a long hatch for serving customers. He took electricity from the pump room to power fridges and freezers. He took water from the pool supply and ran it into the bar to feed a large sink for washing up and a smaller one for hand washing. They managed to beg or borrow fridges and freezers from bars and campsites that were refurbishing. They scavenged a few plastic tables and chairs to put outside the new bar. The end result was a rustic bar by the pool.

At the other end of the pool house Sean took two pipes off the water supply, one directly to a mixer, the other went up to the roof and zigzagged across it and then back to the other side of the mixer to give some solar hot water. Then having mounted two showerheads on the wall and put down a couple of duckboards; the showers were ready too.

They opened for the May Day Holiday and were soon over eighty per cent full, all naturists. It was mid-July before the first textile campers started arriving. A few changed their minds about staying, turned around and left. Some stayed but remained clothed. Others progressively joined the naturists, becoming more clothes casual as time passed.

In the middle of August, Sean and Gill suddenly realised they had not worn clothes for nearly three months, apart from when they were going to suppliers to restock the bar and the snack bar, that had suddenly sort of happened!

The Hernandez' came back at the end of the month, saw all was going well and left them to it. The income from the bars was enough for Sean and Gill, and the Hernandez bank account was getting more income now than ever before, and they were doing nothing.

Sr. Hernandez offered them the house for the winter again. Sean and Gill made small changes and renovated the shower and toilet blocks. They patched hedges and mended fences. There was plenty to keep them busy.

The following May started the same way, busy. Then came a series of surprises. The Hernandez' had decided since the Senora's leg was never going to be right, they were selling up.

"That's wonderful we do all that work and what do we get nothing. Next time we get our own place." Gill was very upset. She dressed and cycled off into town, to be out of the way until she calmed down. While she was out, she bought five lines on the lottery, something she only did when she was feeling very low.

The next morning an e-mail arrived with the news that Gill's mother had been diagnosed with breast cancer. They immediately started packing, Sean got on the phone to Sr. Hernandez telling him they had plane tickets for Saturday and that he needed to sort out replacement staff by then. The Hernandez' decided to come back themselves to allow more time to get replacement staff.

Friday evening, as they ate their last naked Spanish meal, they put the TV on for the lottery draw. They never finished that meal. They were too busy looking at the ticket Gill had bought. They could afford their own business now. They could have bought out the Hernandez' and kept all the rewards for their efforts.

They decided that Gill's mother was more important; claimed the prize and went home to the UK.

They had bought the Eden Gardens Sun Club from the struggling membership committee. By promising a range of good deals for existing members on membership rates, ground rentals and prices on the new projected mobile homes and by promising it would stay a naturist space, the Cutters had got the site at a great price.

They had gone to the bank for the money to build a hard standing and to put in electricity, water and drainage for the mobile home park. The security on offer was far in excess of the loan and the business plan looked comprehensive. The bank granted them the loan. It was only when he read about the planning approval did the bank manager discover that they were funding a naturist resort. Being a shrewd businessman himself, the bank being well protected by the equity in the site, he decided to say nothing about it. He also recognised that his clients' business would be sheltered in a niche market. No one was going to steal their customers. All would be good, just as long as there were enough customers.

That had been ten years ago. The Cutters had extended the loan for a pool refurbishment. Then for the modernisation of the clubhouse and the new terrace. The payments on the loans were always made on time. The bank was very happy with them, although there was no longer a manager at the branch.

Gill's mother was one of the growing number of breast cancer survivors.

☐

Stake Out

Addy then phoned Bea and told her that he had the go-ahead to implement their stakeout plan. Then he told her about the invitation from Sean. Her happy laughter filled his ears.

"I hope you got their permission to do this in plain clothes," she laughed, "You do realise that most of the other people will be naked?" Adding mentally to herself 'That includes me too of course.'

That evening was the first time Bea had seen Addy out of uniform, well uniform trousers. He looked rather smart in his rugby shirt and chinos. He escorted her over to the clubhouse. The Policeman dressed in clothes that you could wear to the pub, her in something less than most pubs would allow. In the clubhouse, it was warm and noisy, the social was a fiftieth birthday party for one of the members and she had lots of friends. By the time the meal had been served most of the guests were naked, or nearly so, and were dancing to an 'Oldies but Goldies' disco. Addy thought it all seemed like fun, but he had work to do. Taking a flask of coffee, he went and sat in his car and watched for activity near the bins. It was about 11:00 pm. Most of the party guests, now fully dressed, had left. When the car door opened and Bea slipped into the passenger side of the car.

"How's it going?" she asked, passing him a sandwich and a can of diet coke.

"Nothing moving over there. That was a nice evening; I'd like to do that again."

"Even with the dress code?"

"What dress code?"

She squeezed his knee then climbed out of the car and disappeared towards her chalet.

The slightly dazed Addy continued his watch.

At 1 am, Bea returned to the car, opened the door and said, "Time to go home."

On Wednesday, they shared a takeaway and then went to the clubhouse for a drink before Addy repeated the previous evening's lookout. The hours passed and nobody came to the bins. Maybe the guys in CID weren't telling lies when they told the younger uniforms that a stakeout was like watching Arsenal and Stoke as they played out a nil-nil match on a wet,

Wednesday night in January. Boring and uncomfortable.

Then Bea came with a warm cup of fresh coffee to tell him it was time to knock off and go home for the night.

On Thursday they varied the routine, Bea sat in the car and chatted with him all evening. Sadly, nobody showed up to try to pick up the booty. A very sad Addy drove home that evening. He had failed to make an arrest. His golden path to CID was fading. He did not know how he was going to continue his relationship with Bea.

The Big Break Through

Bea was distraught, tossing and turning in bed. What was going to happen? Was she ever going to see PC Cutie Pants again? Still sleepless, she was awake early and heard the bin men driving along the road. They always called early to avoid the naturists. She reached for her phone to see what the time was and dropped it. She scrabbled for her phone, like she had PC Cutie Pants' phone under the rubbish bin, the noises she had heard on the night of the break-in ....

Grabbing the blue tracksuit that she always kept in the bedroom, "suppose there is a fire or something" her mum had said. Bea dashed down the road as she zipped up her top. Capturing her breath, she stood still to watch the bins being moved, picked up by the truck and emptied, then pushed back into place.

The bin man moved the bin that the booze had been hidden in and there, underneath it, was a phone.

"STOP!" She shouted in a commanding voice. The bin man stood still almost too scared to move, while the driver looked from the truck window.

How to manage this? After all, the bin men had a job to do. She needed to capture the evidence of how and where the phone had been found. Phone! … Yes of course! Her phone had a camera that would do it.

"OK guys, you see that phone?" she continued in her best I'm-the-woman-in-charge voice, "Do not touch it, leave it exactly where it is. It might be evidence in a burglary case," she explained. "What I want you to do is stand close to the phone while I take a picture to show where it was. It might be a clue in a theft we had here earlier in the week. I might need you to confirm how we found this if it gets to go to court. Then work carefully around it please."

After taking the pictures, she phoned Addy.

"PC Cutie Pants … Get yourself down here pronto!"

"It is 7:30, I was still…"

"Get here now if you want that job in CID, I'll be at the gate in twenty minutes to let you in," and with that, Bea rang off. She stayed to take more photos of activity around the phone as the rest of the bins were emptied.

Some eighteen minutes later, Addy arrived at the gate dressed in a blue tracksuit that matched Bea's, not that either of them noticed.

"Quick, down to the bins!" Shouted Bea, as she jumped in the car, "I've found something."

'Frankly, I don't care,' thought Addy, 'any excuse to be near you first thing in the morning.'

At the bins, Bea pointed to where the phone rested, undisturbed by the bin men. Addy went back to his car for a pair of evidence gloves and an evidence bag. He picked up the phone and put it into the bag. Then turning to Bea, he picked her up in his arms and danced for joy.

Back at the chalet, over a coffee, they examined the phone in its plastic bag. The battery was flat.

"Ah well, we have the skills to recharge it and get it opened at the station, but it would be good to have an idea what was on it before I go making a big deal out of having found it."

"Look there though," pointing at the side of the phone Bea was getting excited, "a micro-SD card slot like the one on my phone. There may be stuff there we can see."

Addy carefully manoeuvred the phone in the plastic bag until he was able to use Bea's eyebrow tweezers to remove the card. He then used the tweezers to put the card in the now empty slot in Bea's phone.

Taking over, because she knew her phone's operating system, Bea checked the e-mail – blank.

Text messages – blank.

Phonebook – blank.

"Looks like all that stuff is in the phone's memory," she muttered to herself.

Photographs – gold! Pictures lots of them. The most recent one was Bea, naked surrounded by her books. The previous one, a different naked woman, then another and another. Then another that looked familiar to Addy, but he didn't know why. The next image was of Gill and the birthday girl from Tuesday, chattering to each other as they walked past the clubhouse. A busy camera where no camera was supposed to be!

Addy was horrified, not by the pictures, but by what would happen to them at the station. What would it mean for the relationship he hoped to have with Bea, if all his mates had seen pictures of her naked? Perhaps it would be better if the phone went to the station without the memory card.

"This is tricky," he explained to Bea, "If I hand it in it for them to do forensics on it, they will find the pictures. I'm sure you and the other people don't want them going public, even within the station. Some of my colleges could get funny about them."

He went on to explain that the Forensics would work out that there should be a memory card in the phone and that would cause trouble for him. Evidence that had been tampered with would be inadmissible in court.

"I think we need to involve Sean in the decision," Bea suggested. "He will have a better understanding of the needs of the members."

"That makes sense," agreed Addy. "He could even decide not to pursue a prosecution if he felt it was not in the Resort's or the members' interest."

Using the tweezers, Addy switched the card back into the slot in the suspect's phone.

Eventually, they tracked Sean down, in the pool house. Where else was Sean going to be at that time in the morning? They explained the nature of the pictures they had seen. They discussed the possible potential implications if some of the less sensitive members of the force got to find out who was enjoying themselves at the Eden Gardens resort.

Sean thought for a few minutes. Then asked Addy if he would leave the phone with him for a couple of hours so that he could get the forensics done privately and confidentially by an expert. "That will mean, of course, you need to be out of the way when this is happening, to protect the expert," he added.

This caused Addy to pause and think again.

At this point, Bea piped up, "Suppose I didn't know your phone number and had found a lost phone, who would I have given it to?"

Addy's face brightened, "Well, I'm not actually on duty until this afternoon, Friday night is a busy one for us, so the Rota is built to get as many of us on duty as possible. Maybe you didn't phone me and I haven't yet seen this evidence." He turned to Sean, "Your expert is a professional I take it?"

"I'll tell you what, I'll go and call them now and see how they feel about this. I'm certain they will say if it won't work and then we are on to a non-starter." Sean picked up his mobile and wandered out to the poolside, almost out of earshot. From that distance, they could hear only the odd word as Sean explained the situation.

"Why didn't you say you weren't on duty when I called, instead of driving over here like a lunatic, look at you, you're not even dressed!"

"Bea, when you called you sounded so excited I just had to come," replied Addy. "Besides, I had to get up anyway."

"The phone was ringing," they finished the old joke together. Addy watched her eyes dance, as they both tried to suppress their laughter.

"While we are on the subject of your early morning phone call, what is this 'PC Cutie Pants' thing you called me?"

"That is just the name I use for you," the eyes were dancing with the smile again.

At that point, Sean returned, "All sorted, my expert will be here in about half an hour and reckons it will take a couple of hours to do a professional job of gathering as much info as possible without a full IT Suite. So, can you both make yourselves scarce, go into town shopping or something?"

As he drove towards his flat, Addy was in a great mood, and then a thought crossed his mind,

"Why did Sean automatically send the two of us away?"

"Oh! PC Cutie Pants, you are supposed to be the observant gatherer of intelligence. I suppose he thinks he has seen enough circumstantial evidence to classify us as a couple?"

"What is with that 'PC Cutie Pants' stuff again?" asked Addy, choosing to ignore the fact that his dearest, secret wish had been tumbled by some else so quickly.

"OK, I'll explain if you make me a cup of coffee while you are getting changed."

Despite ten minutes of teasing and silly threats, it wasn't until Bea had her cup of coffee that she began to explain.

"Firstly, the only name you have been introduced to me by is PC Adiscombe, but that would be rather formal don't you think?"

Addy nodded.

"You have told me that your colleagues call you Addy, but I am not going to be your colleague, now or ever. I do think that you are cute, and have done ever since you managed our first meeting without staring."

Addy smiled at the thought of her thinking he was cute.

"In the time, I have known you, apart from this morning, you have nearly always been in uniform or at least part of it. You have always had trousers on, or as they say in America pants." She switched into an American accent and stretched the 'a' sound to emphasise the difference between the English pants and the American. "and there you are, PC Cutie Pants!"

Addy laughed. "OK. No uniform this morning. Where do you fancy, the new shopping centre or the old High Street?"

"Well Cutie Pants, perhaps the High Street, there is a nice new cake shop I'd love to have a look at."

"Ok, give me ten minutes while I get some better clothes on and we'll be off," Addy climbed to his feet.

"Cutie Pants?"

"Yes?"

"Is there another name I can call you by?"

"I am not telling you my given name. I suppose my Mum will when you meet her, she likes it. She is the one who gave it to me."

"OK. I'll stick to PC Cutie Pants until something new comes along," she called back. 'Hmm, I'm going to meet his Mum! He is planning on sticking around,' Bea mused, as a sudden thrill ran through her. She hugged herself as she finished her drink.

A few minutes later, with both of them now dressed for a Friday morning on the town, an event Addy was planning to enjoy as much as any Friday night on the town, he led them both out of the flat. The door shut behind them with a resounding crash. That made Addy grin, he might just be involved with a woman who didn't do quiet exits.

Bea had two objectives for the morning besides the cake shop. The first was to sort out a new phone to replace the clunker PCCP, not that that was any better by way of a nickname, was using. The other was to get to know her man in an off-duty setting.

The phone took a while to sort out; several times they had both wondered out loud, why are phone shops so slow? Eventually, they emerged with a phone identical to Bea's, but with a black case, rather than the princess pink number that hers sported. Addy had settled for that model so that he could call his personal help desk when he needed guidance through the screens. Something he expected to have to do often.

Over coffee and cakes, it was a good cake shop, they swapped favourite songs, singers, pet hates and football teams. The football teams nearly caused a fight, until they discovered that actually, neither of them had any real interest in soccer. Bea had only chosen her team for the purpose of teasing her brothers and Addy revealed he definitely preferred rugby to soccer. So, instead of disagreeing, they laughed.

"You will have something in common with my Dad when you meet him then." It was Addy's turn to thrill at the thought of taking their relationship to the next level.

Bea felt she was making progress towards her final objective.

Despite the early start to the day, it was after lunch by the time they got back to Eden Gardens. They quickly located Sean and the phone in the bar.

"The good news first," said Sean and he went on to explain that his expert had taken a good set of prints from the phone and a nice thumbprint on the memory card. That would link the pictures to the user of the phone. The phone battery was indeed flat but recharging it had been easy. "It seems almost everyone has one of these phones nowadays. So my charger did the job."

Addy shook his head at that and smiled a wry smile.

"Now we get to the really good news. How many people use 1, 2, 3, 4 as their PIN do you think? Well, lado was one of the one in ten who do!" Continued Sean.

Addy now had the subject for his first call to the help desk, how to change that code from the pre-set pin of four zeros.

Sean went on, explaining what the expert had found out about the use of the phone. The phone book didn't contain anything useful, lots of numbers but all were for Gboy, AP or some similar name. They had moved on to look at the call history. This was far more revealing.

From about half-past one on Monday morning, there were ten unanswered calls from a local phone number. A couple from another mobile and after half-past ten Monday, nothing. At this time, the Expert had suggested, the battery went flat.

"So, is there actually any bad news?" Asked Addy.

"Well, sort of," began Sean, as he explained that there were two issues. The first was, as Bea had already suggested, that both he and his expert were of the opinion that these photos were too sensitive to go through the hands of the police. Some people featured in them might find explaining them away to a wider population somewhat difficult.

The second issue was that Sean had recognised the landline number.

Three, maybe four years ago, Eden Gardens had a bit of bother with a planning application. He explained how a developer had wanted to build a number of three-floor townhouses in a field close to the boundary of the Resort. Sean had, of course, objected to the application and had done a bit of canvassing for support amongst the local councillors for the ward. He had managed to build quite a good rapport with Councillor Harper and she had, by and large, been supportive of the Resort and its objection to the plans. In the end, the plans were dropped and some bungalows had been built instead.

"This is Councillor Harper's number," he concluded.

Going Off Piste

"I see your difficulty with this," announced Bea, "There must be a way around it."

"One thing that is clear, we can't let this go to court," Sean stated very clearly, "I can't afford to have both members of the council and the club up in arms against us!"

Addy had been quiet for a long time, he shifted on his seat the other two looked towards him.

"Call me daft, but I have the feeling that Councillor Harper would not have climbed over your wall in a pair of size nine Nike trainers, or worn-out Doc Martins, to take pictures of naked people, mainly women, and then break in and steal money and spirits from the bar?"

Bea and Sean looked at each other and nodded.

"As a Councillor she could have asked to visit and you would probably have drowned her in drinks and offered a large contribution to her re-election campaign fund to be assured of her continued support," he continued with a smile, "Well you would have done if you were in America!"

"True, we would have extended her our best hospitality," admitted Sean.

"And more!" added Gill who had just arrived. "It sounds more like teenage boys to me."

Addy agreed.

"What else do we know about Councillor Harper's household?" He asked.

"I'll look up her profile on the Council website," said Sean, as he flipped open his phone.

A few minutes of frantic tapping followed. During this pause, Addy imagined just how good it would feel to do that sort of thing for himself when the need arose. Some one-to-one tuition from his helpdesk service might be called for. Sean found what he was looking for and he started to read.

"Married to Brian with two children both of whom attend the local comprehensive school."

"Well, that could see them in our age range, couldn't it?"

"Very true, Gill, but it doesn't say what sex they are or anything," Sean was getting frustrated.

"What about Facebook? Does she have a profile there?" Gill wasn't about to give up at the first obstacle.

A few more minutes of tapping.

"Sorry, a great idea but no Facebook, I'll try a Google search." Sean started tapping. "Several results." More tapping, "Ah, here is her prospectus for the last election and there is a picture of the family with, and he read the caption: "Husband Brian and sons Martin (14) and Peter (12),"

Sean fell silent.

"A bit young then," said Gill. The Co-Owners of the resort looked crestfallen. Bea looked at Addy and saw him starting to smile.

"Sean," he started, "The last election must have been almost three years ago; it was before I moved back here. Meaning we have a 17 or 15-year-old boy with access to that phone." Addy paused to let that sink in. "I know you don't want to take this to court and you have the drink back, so at the moment, there is the damage to the door and just shy of £300 in cash outstanding… Plus, the improperly obtained photos. Am I right?"

Sean and Gill nodded.

"If I can get the perpetrators to come here and apologise to you, and maybe the members, you might be willing to drop the case?"

More nodding from Sean and Gill.

"And if they are willing to do a bit of… let's call it 'restitution work' they might get the phone back – with a wiped memory card of course?"

"That would be a great trick if you can pull it off," Sean was all smiles now.

"Yes please," from Gill.

"I'll need to take the phone with me and I have to get to work." Addy got to his feet and made his farewells.

The next few hours saw Addy undertaking his normal duties. Before it was time to go out in the car on patrol he had time to join in the banter with his colleagues. He was surprised his mates had not rumbled his frequent visits to Eden Gardens. Amazingly, it appeared that the day shift had not seen him escorting an attractive trainee solicitor around town either.

He had reported to his Superiors that nobody had come to collect the hidden Scotch. Before his watch last night, he had spoken to Mr Cutter. He was pleased to be able to say that Mr Cutter was glad to have some of his property back and was happy that the police had done their best. Meanwhile, in the back of his mind, he was running a lot of different scenarios for the conversation he was hoping to have later that evening with Councillor Harper. It always amazed him how, in these conversations, as he rehearsed them, slight changes in wording appeared to have big effects on the outcome.

Early Friday evening is always quiet. The blood alcohol levels in a hundred or more young men and girls slowly rising as they drank themselves towards bursting point. Sometime tonight all that alcohol would explode into shouts and screams, pushing and pulling, punching and kicking, bleeding but, hopefully for the parents of the town, no dying. Addy and every other officer on duty, in every town in the country, would be doing their best to stop the escalation of violence beyond the shouting and screaming. This week like every week, they would fail and some youngsters will be going home from their Friday night out via the overstretched A&E service.

At about half-past six, Addy called in that he was having a break and got the all-clear from the control room. He was parked by the kerb, outside a smart, what he guessed was a four-bedroomed house in a quiet residential street. He got out and walked up the path to the front door, noting that there were two cars, both small hatchbacks, on the drive. He pressed the bell push and the classic ding-dong rang inside. A few moments later, the door was opened by a woman dressed in a skirt and pullover and about 70 years old. Addy was a little taken back by this unexpected development.

"Good evening, how may I help you Officer?" she enquired.

"I wondered if Councillor Harper was at home? I wanted to talk to her, about a private matter. It is quite urgent."

In the protracted conversation that followed, he discovered that he was talking to the Councillor's mother-in-law. The councillor was away on a short trip to France with her husband. They had asked her to stay in the house and keep an eye on the boys while they were away. The Harper's plane from Bordeaux was due in at Gatwick quite early, so they should be home by lunchtime tomorrow. He thanked her for her help, wished her a pleasant evening and found himself being told about the viewing options for the night on TV.

As he walked back to his car, he thought about how much easier the job would be if everyone was so open when you asked a simple question. Then he smiled to himself as the idea that, with all that chatter, it might take even longer to get the same result danced through his imagination.

Then Friday night got started. He caught a drunk driver as she was on her way to a nightclub.

"I only had a couple of vodkas to get me started." The young girl was dressed in even less than most of the naturists at Eden Gardens had been wearing when he interviewed them.

"You tell him, Babes," encouraged her companions. Boobs bulging out of their tops, bellies over their waistbands. He was certain that a couple of them were either in thongs or commando under, no, make that behind, their skirts.

As Babes was put in the back of a van to be taken to the station for processing, her mates staggered off, tottering on their stiletto heels complaining about the ''kin Pigs, spoiling our fun'. As if being mangled and scarred in a car crash caused by their drunken driver was going to be the highlight

72

of their lives. Addy shook his head and arrange for the tow truck to take the car to the lockup.

By ten that evening, the 'Start the Weekend Party' at Eden Gardens was in full swing, the bar was busy and the disco was playing a selection of 70's hits and a few people were dancing. At the tables around the dance floor, people were holding shouted conversations. Bea was telling her mother and father about her interesting week. Before midnight, most people started heading off into the night calling out to their friends and laughing at old jokes retold.

As the witching hour slipped past, Bea and her parents retired to Grandma's and were sipping a nightcap while making plans for the morning.

Just before half-past one, it kicked off in town. Two groups of drunken girls had bumped into each other as they moved from one club to another. Handbags and hair pulling led to the boyfriends getting involved with each other. When the Police arrived at first in dribs and drabs, then a full stick, both groups turned on the police. Being sober, trained and coordinated, the police soon had the situation under control. The ambulances arrived and the bleeding were taken to the Accident & Emergency unit where overworked doctors and nurses waited for the abuse and assaults the weekend too often brings.

At three o'clock in the morning, Addy was stood down and went home to get some sleep.

Addy woke, as the sun shone through his window, it was nearly ten. He reached for his new phone. There was a text from Bea.

"How did it go yesterday? B xxx"

Three kisses! He wished Bea had come to deliver them in person. Three whole kisses. Long, passionate kisses.

"Stop it, you'll go blind." He reprimanded himself, wondering if he could stop at the needing glasses stage. Instead, he got out of bed and went for a shower.

Addy called Bea. Over the next twenty minutes, he explained the outcome of yesterday's call on the Councillor. His plan for the day. His plans for Sunday and Monday. Although in fact, he had no plans for his days off that he wouldn't change at the drop of a hat. He wanted to get to know Bea better and he was going to do whatever he had to do to succeed in that goal.

Two pm saw an off-duty Addy back on Councillor Harper's doorstep. He pressed the doorbell. It was answered by a woman he immediately recognised from the internet pictures as the Councillor. The holiday had obviously suited her she looked tanned and relaxed. She was dressed in dark blue slacks and a turquoise polo shirt with a logo saying, "La Jenny", just above her left breast.

"Good Afternoon Councillor," started Addy, holding up his warrant card. "I am PC Adiscombe, I need to talk to you about a rather private matter."

The Councillor took Addy through to the lounge. As they entered, a man, dressed in a similar polo top, stood up to leave. Addy guessed this was Brian Harper, and suggested that it would be best if he stayed, as he would probably have an interest in the matter Addy needed to discuss too. To break the ice, he asked about the holiday leading with, "Are the shirts from your trip to France?"

The slightly hesitant response was, "Well, yes they are from the place we stayed at."

Seeing this softly, softly approach was going to cause more difficulty, Addy decided to concentrate on a factual explanation of the situation. He put the phone they had recovered at the resort, on the coffee table in front of the Harpers. Then he started with the story of the burglary and the subsequent investigation. He then asked them if they recognised the phone. Both the Harpers looked at each other and admitted that the phone looked like their younger son, Peter's, phone. When Addy gave them the phone's number, the shocked couple just looked at each other. Addy continued to detail what had been found on the memory card. They were horrified. Addy told them the other number that had called the lost phone and they look as if their world had collapsed. It was Martin's number. They were both involved in it.

Addy then told them about Mr Cutter's concerns. That he was worried about not damaging the reputations of the members of the resort and the reputation of the Resort itself. He told them Mr Cutter valued their friendship and the support for the Resort that the Harpers had given.

Addy explained to avoid collateral damage to all concerned, Mr and Mrs Cutter would be prepared to let the matter rest, subject to a couple of conditions. Addy then outlined his plan for restitutional justice. The Harper's looked happier, they asked for a few minutes to talk in private and went into another room. Addy looked around the comfortable family room. He noticed a picture of two boys, sitting on their bikes, that stood on the mantelpiece; the two villains! They just didn't look the part. At that moment, the Harpers returned. Mr Harper stood squarely behind his wife with his hands on her shoulders. The Councillor told

Addy that, if the boys knew what was best for them, they would be at the resort to make a public apology tomorrow, Sunday.

They then surprised Addy by asking if he could arrange for them to have a table for four for lunch in the clubhouse afterwards.

A more than slightly confused Addy agreed to pass on the booking request to Mr Cutter while he was conveying the outcome of his visit.

Before he went on duty for Saturday night, Addy phoned Sean and told him about the apology offer and the table booking. Sean said he would reserve the table and arrange for the Harpers to be admitted to the grounds.

After that, Addy called Bea and over the next hour explained what had happened at the Harper's, and the table booking. Bea astutely inquired about the Harpers' French holiday trip. Addy said his attempt to use it as an icebreaker had gone wrong, but they were both wearing holiday souvenir T-shirts, with a 'La Jenny' logo. Bea had laughed and suggested that he came to lunch on Sunday too; it was a special day in the Resort's calendar. The official pool opening.

Saturday night was less explosive than Friday night had been. Addy was finished soon after one o'clock and went home for a good long sleep. He looked at his phone, as he got ready for bed. There was a text from Bea. He read her reminder that lunch was from mid-day, and not to dress for the event. There were another three kisses. He smiled as he went to sleep.

Restitutional Justice

Sunday dawned sunny and warm. Addy woke up with that smile still on his face. He dressed in a pair of chino jeans and a polo shirt. He ate a light breakfast of strawberry yoghurt and a piece of toast, washed down with a cup of his usual black coffee. He, in truth, didn't like white coffee but had learnt to drink it to be polite. Around half-past ten, he got in the car and headed off to his date with Bea!

Bea met him at the gate of Eden Gardens, jumped into his car, leaned over and gave him a kiss on the cheek. They drove through the gate to the car parking area. He parked in a space between two other cars.

"May I?" He asked, as he reached across to Bea and pulled her gently to him and planted a kiss on her lips.

"You most certainly can," Bea re-engaged lips. This time, the kiss lasted longer and was far more passionate. Addy's hand moved from behind Bea's back and cupped her naked breast. Simultaneously they realised that they needed to get out of the car and get a little bit of air. Both were happy that their relationship was now openly that of lovers. Both were looking forward to taking their intimacy further. Both knew that sitting in a car, in the carpark of a naturist resort was not the appropriate place for it.

Addy could see the golden flecks in the chocolate brown eyes shimmer as the eyes danced and the face smiled. What he didn't know was Bea could see almost the same thing happening on his face.

Holding hands, they walked towards Grandma's Summer Place. As they walked, Bea explained that lunch today was going to be on the terrace of the clubhouse. It was a tradition that on the first warm Sunday of the year, most of the members and the few guests would eat lunch there and afterwards, at three o'clock, there would be a mass splash down when everybody would jump in the pool. Which, thanks to the solar water heating put in a few years back, and the nice weather all week, was showing as twenty-two degrees already.

The reason why this hadn't happened last weekend was down to the weather forecast on Wednesday not being that good for the following Sunday. As usual, the forecasters had it wrong, the heavy showers forecast had arrived on Saturday and Sunday had been nice enough to enjoy a few hours in the pool in the afternoon.

"There is one more thing," Bea added, as she opened the gate to the chalet. An older couple, both naked of course, stood as Addy entered. "Mum, Dad this is PC Adiscombe. He has been helping to sort out last weekend's crime wave."

Barry and Sylvia Johnston didn't believe that was all there was for a second. They had seen the body language at the gate to Grandma's Summer Place. They were glad to see their daughter happy, even if she wanted to delay telling them the full story. They made their excuses, picked up their towels and went to talk to their friends down by the miniten courts.

"Miniten courts?" enquired Addy.

"Later," she steered him indoors.

As lunchtime approached, it occurred to Addy that Councillor Harper, her husband and her children would all be at lunch. What should he wear? The turquoise polo shirts that Addy had described had given Bea a very strong hint.

"How about nothing? Wrap your towel around you and we will keep discreetly off to one side out of the line of sight. Then when the Harpers have finished, if you feel comfortable, lose the towel."

So, Bea had it all planned out. Secretly Addy had hoped there would be a way to remain inconspicuous. However, he desperately wanted to be a part of Bea's life and if that meant joining in with naturist events, bring it on! Just if it got out that he was a naturist, it could make his life as a policeman difficult and to have the Councillor see him at a naturist event might speed that up.

Still, with his towel wrapped firmly around his waist, holding onto Bea's left hand (she held her towel in her right), they walked to the clubhouse. Bea slipped away for a few minutes to explain to Sean and Gill that Addy was 'undercover' and not to draw attention to him.

Addy spent those minutes sitting at a table off to one side of the terrace trying to be inconspicuous. He looked around at the amazing variety of bodies that came into sight and tried hard not to stare. There were men and women of all ages and a few children. There were tanned bodies and pale bodies. There were tall people and short people. There were hairy people and bald people, in more ways than one! None of the bodies looked like a movie star, except the person talking to Sean and Gill. People chatting with each other, people with a drink in their hand, laughing at each other's jokes. Nobody in sight was having sex…

Just then, a large estate car pulled into the car park. Four people got out. An adult couple, he was dressed in smart shorts and a loose-fitting shirt, her in a pale blue sundress. With them were two teenage boys in baggy jeans and rumpled T-shirts proclaiming the latest bands. The Harpers had arrived as promised.

Sean went to meet them. He shook hands with the two adults and offered his hand to the two teenagers. Reluctantly each, in turn, took it and briefly shook. Sean led them over to the stage. He picked up a microphone, standing in front of the family; he called for silence.

"Last weekend, these two boys did some rather silly things. They are here today as grownups to apologise for their actions. Please listen respectfully to what they have to say."

Martin, the elder of the two, took the microphone.

"Last weekend we climbed over the fence into this place and took some pictures of you. We were going to share them with our mates. This was wrong. After doing that, we broke into the clubhouse and stole some money and stuff. That was wrong too."

He handed the microphone to Peter. The younger brother continued their apology.

"If we hadn't dropped the phone with the pictures on it, we would have shared the pictures. We would have sold the stuff and we would have spent the money. Instead, the Police found the phone and told Mum and Dad about it. They were hurt by what we had done and that was wrong too."

All eyes were fixed on the two lads on the stage.

"We can't make what we did right, but the pictures have been destroyed, the stuff returned and we have the money with us. It is just the hurt that remains. We would both like to apologise to you all for our silly actions, to Mr and Mrs Cutter for the damage and worry we caused and to Mum and Dad for letting them down."

"Yes, we are both very sorry," added the elder boy, as their parents, both now naked, walked up to the very embarrassed boys and gave them a group hug. So captivating had the boys' apology been nobody had noticed when the two adults, standing off to one side of the stage, slipped out of their clothes. The club members gathered in the restaurant stood up and applauded. First the two boys and when they saw the transformation, the whole family. Gill came over from the bar with an arm full of towels for the Harpers.

During lunch, Addy, still dressed in his undercover clothing went to the bar for more drinks. As he approached, the woman in front of him turned to go back to her table, he found himself face-to-face with the naked Councillor Harper. She smiled in recognition. Gave him a wink and a nod of understanding. Then walked back to the table she was sharing with her family, and, as and when they had a few seconds off, Sean and Gill.

Addy carried the fresh classes back to his table, slid the drinks to Bea and her Mum and Dad and put his down. Then he undid the towel around his waist, dropped it on his chair and sat on it. Thus finished Addy's first undercover operation.

"What happened while you were away to cause that change?" Bea asked.

"Something the Councillor didn't say when we almost bumped into each other, I think!" Then the dessert arrived.

After the sticky toffee pudding and custard, they continued to chat about places they had visited and shows they had seen. It turned out that both Dad and Addy preferred rugby to soccer and they had been on the same coach to Twickenham to see England being beaten by Wales the year before last.

☐

The Big Splash

A bell sounded! As one the assembled crowd leapt to their feet and ran towards the pool. It was three o'clock already! As soon as they reached the pool, everybody jumped straight in. The water was fresh. Addy felt bits of his skin thrill at the sensation of the cool water. As he broke the surface, he knew he never wanted to swim in clothes of any sort ever again.

He looked around, and there was Bea, climbing out of the pool, water streaming down her, already-tanned, body. "At least I still have a bit of a tan from my holiday in the Canaries at Easter," Addy thought, "unlike some of the paler people." He felt so good he sank to the bottom again just for the sheer indulgent pleasure of it. This was the best day of his life. He was in love with a beautiful woman and she loved him, now he was free; floating in the clear cool water, looking up at the blue sky on the first day of June. The first day of a new life.

He moved over to the steps and climbed out. That felt good too, no saggy, baggy costume clinging wet around his bits. "I could get to like this skinny-dipping!"

"Over here Cottontail," he heard Bea's Dad's voice and saw him waving his redundant undercover clothing.

He turned and walked over to where Bea's family were spread out on their towels, drying in the sun. Addy took his towel and spread it out too, and sat down to dry off.

"Why did you call out Cottontail to attract my attention just now?" He asked Bea's Dad.

"Cottontail is a term used by naturists to describe someone with a tanned body and a white bum like a cottontail rabbit!" laughed Dad and Mum.

Bea looked thoughtful, "What was that old kid's programme you made us watch last Christmas Dad? The one on the DVD we got you. Ah, I remember it's all right." She smiled, the golden flecks in her eyes danced.

She turned to Addy and in her best vicar's voice intoned, "In the presence of this congregation of naked people, I hereby name thee 'Rags' and all naturists throughout the land will rejoice to call you thus." She laughed and kissed him.

Addy still looked confused, so Bea explained that naturists normally only used nicknames, because as Addy (or was he now Rags?) had found, many people who were naturists did not want to be identified as such outside of naturist circles. The risk of this happening was reduced by avoiding the use of family names. For example, there are lots of Micks, but only one Mick Jagger!

"Ah," thought Rags to himself, "that is why I had to be Cutie Pants!" He kissed Bea again, and in a loud voice announced, "I accept the name Rags to be the name by which, henceforth, all naturists throughout the land shall know me!"

A ragged cheer went up from the people relaxing around them. Rags went red. Bea and her parents burst out laughing. The people who had cheered now applauded. To hide his embarrassment Addy, or was he Rags, dived back into the pool.

"This is so nice, I am going to be Rags for Bea and for the joy of skinny-dipping," he thought, as the water rushed past his whole body again. He surfaced and found himself face-to, well almost, -face with Councillor Harper.

"Rags, please call me Elaine now we are to be friends, come over and have a drink with Brian and me. We are about to go and get a coffee and some soft drinks for the boys. Bring your charming friend with you too." With that, she pulled herself out of the water and walked back to her family.

As she went Rags noticed that she did not have a cottontail, but had an even tan from top to toe. He fished himself out of the water, found his towel and dried himself off.

"Welcome to our naturist family, I'm Barry or Baz, and my wife is Sylvie," said Bea's Dad, introducing themselves by name for the first time.

"I think I'm going to enjoy being part of this family," replied Rags, not quite to himself. He was unsure of which family he was pleased with being welcomed into. Both Baz and Sylvie were hoping he meant their family, the Johnstons. They could not remember seeing Bea looking so happy and relaxed in years. They were also happy with the idea Rags sounded like he wanted to be part of the family of naturism too. It was so much a part of their family life, that rejection of this could have created a terrible strain within the Johnston family.

Addy put the damp towel over his shoulder and turned to Bea,

"Coun... sorry, Elaine and Brian have just asked us to go and have a coffee or something with them."

"That's nice," Bea said, standing up and picking up her towel, "back soon," she added to her parents. They walked side by side across the lawn.

"Don't they just make a lovely couple? I do so hope it works out," sighed Sylvie to no one in particular.

"Aye, I'm with you on that love," and Barry closed his eyes for a few minutes, just to check his eyelids were working right.

Barry Remembers

Behind his closed eyelids, Barry's mind rolled back to how he had met Sylvie. He was just twenty-three and a big, strong, young man. He was near to finishing his training as a bricklayer. Life was looking good. Then, during his regular Saturday afternoon rugby match, a scrum collapsed. He felt his shoulder twist and then a huge wave of pain hit him.

At Casualty, as they called the A&E unit in those days, they told him he had dislocated his shoulder and torn the ligaments badly. A rather pretty nurse popped into his cubicle a few times. Although he hadn't felt much like making conversation, he had noted the name 'Sylvia Edwards', from her badge. After a couple of hours, the doctors decided to have a go at manipulating his shoulder back. Staff Nurse Edwards gave him the mask and told him it was a gas and air mix. He was to take a few breaths and then the doctor would pull and rotate his shoulder back into place. The pain was incredible as his shoulder slipped back into place.

The nurse pulled her hand free from his grip, shook it and said, "That hurt, didn't it?"

Barry could only nod; he knew that if he opened his mouth the tears streaming from his eyes would be joined by unmanly sobs.

They strapped his arm to his body. They gave him a big pot of painkillers and he left with an appointment for the Monday clinic.

On Monday, a very sleep-deprived Barry arrived for his clinic appointment. The strapping was removed from around his arm and pain crashed through his body.

"Not good," said the doctor as Barry winced with every move. "I think your rugby days are over."

Barry walked out of the clinic; the doctor had signed him off work for two weeks and given him a prescription for more painkillers. At the pharmacy, there was a huge wait, so after dropping off his prescription he had gone to the WRVS canteen for a cup of tea and a sandwich. Stood in the queue for the counter, he found himself behind Nurse Edwards.

"Here, let me get that for you, to say sorry for crushing your hand on Saturday."

She had looked round to see who was behind her. Then she had recognised Barry and had smiled at him.

"Thank you that would be nice."

They had sat together and talked about his clinic visit.

"Looks like I'll have some free time Saturday afternoons." He had dug deep into his courage and continued, "I don't suppose I could spend some of it with you?"

She had asked him what he had in mind. Barry had told her that he had no idea what people did on a Saturday afternoon if they weren't playing rugby. He asked what nurses did on their days off.

"I do my washing, go shopping and look forward to the summer," she had replied, with a saucy smile on her face. "We could go and see my brother's band at the White Horse. That's if you like blues-rock?"

Having decided that he liked whatever Nurse Edwards liked, he arranged to meet her at the pub at eight. She had already finished her tea; she thanked him for paying for it and went back to work.

With two weeks, at least, off work, Barry needed something to fill his days. The ideal thing arrived that evening. The neighbour from next door came around with a box of circuit boards, resistors and plastic bits. He explained it was a computer he had bought for his son. The firm he worked for used a computer to do the pay role and to keep the accounts. He believed that computers in offices and homes were the next big thing. He had bought the Sinclair ZX80 to try to get his son interested. The problem was, that he had no idea how to put it together. Knowing that Barry was good with his hands and was off work, he wondered if Barry could get it put together?

Barry found the entire project fascinating and spent the next three days building the computer and testing it. He worked through all the examples included in the book that came with the kit, following the instructions step-by-step. It was a shame that these things were of very little real use. Still, it was a wrench when he had to go next door on Thursday evening to return it to its owner.

Friday dragged by, his arm still hurt every time he moved; if he sat still his arm ached. Each hour seemed to last a week. The only thing keeping him going was the thought of Saturday night. He had pestered his mother into washing and ironing his best shirt. His Mum was good to him, she always had his best interests heart, so she washed and pressed his best jeans too.

On Saturday, he went into town. He bought a new pair of trousers and a bottle of aftershave. His mum was pleased with the trousers. "Much better than his jeans," she thought to herself. Unfortunately, the bottle of aftershave slipped out of her hands and smashed on the tiled floor of the kitchen. His mother cleaned up the mess with her new floor cloth. His mother always had his interest at heart, so she wanted her boy to have a nice evening.

Barry had a bath, washed his hair and had a shave. He towelled his hair dry, borrowed his sister's hairdryer, and styled it just so. In his bedroom, he laid out his shirt, new trousers, socks and his lucky … where were they? He went through his chest of drawers, they weren't there. He looked under the bed, no not there either, nor were they in the washing basket. Where were his lucky pants? He double-checked everywhere, but still no sign. Pulling on a pair of tracksuit bottoms, he ran downstairs.

"Mum," he called, "have you seen my best pants anywhere?"

"Which ones are you talking about?" Asked his mum from the kitchen. She was standing at the sink rinsing out her new floor cloth; she always looked after her boy.

Barry arrived at the pub at 7:45. He was wearing his best shirt, new trousers and new underwear. He had decided against using Dad's aftershave. He held the door open for a guy, about his age, who was carrying a large amplifier. He went over to the bar, to order a half of bitter; he wanted to pace himself. Another crash at the door and a drum appeared with a stocky man following close behind. By eight o'clock, the pub was littered with amps, speakers, wires and guitars. The drummer had put his kit together and the rest of the band members were setting up the PA system and the backline.

Nurse Edwards arrived a little later, she went straight to the guy Barry had helped through the door and gave him a hug and a peck on the cheek. Barry felt a lurch inside. Then she saw Barry over at the bar, waved to him and smiling hurried towards him.

"Hello, you," she said smiling, "You came then! I am so glad, I didn't want to have to listen to my brother and his mates on my own again!"

"Of course, I came; I have been looking forward to it all week. What would you like to drink?"

Barry ordered the drinks and carried them to a table. He sat down next to her and winced as he slid her drink across to her.

"Your shoulder still not settling down then?"

"No, I'm still getting a lot of discomfort, how is your hand?" He smiled as she tried to make sense of his question. Then it clicked.

"I had the cast cut off this morning; they think it will regain full function in time!"

They both laughed. Barry smiled, "I have a live one here alright!" He thought to himself.

The band started a soundcheck and conversation had to stop for a few minutes, as the band worked their way through a quick 12-bar blues, adjusting volumes as they went. When they stopped Sylvie's brother came over to their table.

"So, this is the reason you came tonight?" He gestured towards Barry, "Aren't you going to introduce us?"

"Hi, Dave," she turned to Barry, "This is …"

Sensing that she was struggling, Barry stood up and offered his hand. "The name is Barry, Barry Johnston, pleased to meet you, Dave."

"Hey! Dave, what are we going to start with?" The other guitarist called across.

"I'll be right back," said Dave as he left them.

Barry sat down and took a sip of his beer.

"Do I call you Sylvia?" He asked, "I read it on your name badge last week."

"It is my name," she smiled, "You had an advantage over me, you only had a number on your shirt, number 5!"

"Let me correct that then, my name is Barry or Baz Johnston, I am pleased to meet you, Miss Edwards."

Sylvie snorted with laughter and Barry noticed she had dark brown eyes that smiled at him.

"Wah! Please, Mr Johnston, do call me Sylvie." She fluttered a beer mat in front of her face, like a refugee from 'Gone with the Wind.

They stayed for the first half of the evening, the band was pretty good, even if their light show was rather static. Dave joined them at the break, and they talked over a beer, Baz and Dave seemed to hit it off. Sylvia was pleased that she had a date with someone Dave approved of; he had not been keen on the last two disasters.

The second set started and conversation became impossible.

"There is a new Burger Restaurant just opened," he shouted into Sylvie's ear. "Would you like to go and try it?" She nodded and they got up and went to the door, Dave gave a quick thumbs-up, and they went out into the evening.

The following week, Barry popped next door to borrow the computer for a couple of days. He had an idea he wanted to try out. In between hours spent with the computer, he made several trips to the library to look through back copies of electronics magazines. He made several trips to the electronics shop too.

On Thursday, he took a break from his experimentation to take Sylvia out on her day off. At the end of the evening, he walked her home. On the doorstep, Sylvia asked him in. From the minute he stepped across the threshold, his life changed forever.

He was surprised and really glad to only find Dave in the house.

"Mum and Dad are at the club," Dave informed his sister. "Sue has a shift at the pub tonight; I'll be picking her up and going back to her place afterwards"

"Actually, Dave I wanted a word about your light show, do you have any free time tomorrow, I want to show you something?" Barry ventured.

The band had gigs on both Friday and Saturday night but Dave said he would be free on Sunday. With Sylvie being on a night shift on Friday and then on a late shift on Sunday, that seemed to fit for all of them.

Friday, Barry and Sylvia went to the coast for a walk along the beach and fish and chips wrapped in newspaper for lunch. As he drove them back, Barry pulled into a lay-by near a local beauty spot.

On Saturday, they wandered the High Street, they didn't buy anything in particular just window-shopped, they met some friends, talked and laughed. When it was time for Sylvie to get some sleep, Barry took her home.

"Don't listen to everything Dave says tomorrow, he is a real tease at times," Sylvie warned him. Just in case Dave tried to do the brotherly thing and tell whoppers (or even worse, the truth) about his sister!

Sunday afternoon, Barry demonstrated his light controller to Dave. Dave was impressed with the way it worked.

"How did you do it?" Dave asked.

Barry explained that it had a computer driving a load of sound to light and light flashing circuits. He could adjust the sensitivity to the changes in the music with one knob and the speed of changes with another. The hard bit was trying to get it to stop either dark or light when there is no music. He had solved it with a double footswitch one side for dark and one for all on. They chatted for half an hour or so before Dave asked if they could use Barry's magic box. Barry explained that the electrical bits had cost a couple of pounds, but the computer was on loan and he would have to buy a new one. "That'll set us back about seventy quid," he finished.

"Well that is roundabout what we get for a night, so I'll chat to the rest of the band and let you know. I think it would be really good for us and help us get better-paid gigs." With that, Dave went off into the night.

On Monday morning, Barry went back to work. It didn't last long. Tuesday saw him signed off work for another week. His shoulder wasn't up to it yet.

He saw Sylvie a couple of times in the week and she passed on a message from Dave that the band wanted his lighting system. On one of their afternoons together, Barry bought another computer kit.

The man behind the counter of the electrical store asked if he was sure he wanted the kit, lots of people were struggling with them. Barry laughed, "I have already built one and it worked so well I have a commission for a second."

The store owner asked if he would be interested in building a few for his customers.

By the time he went back to the building site, he could put one together in a couple of hours. He had also been in demand to show people how to use them.

When, inevitably, his shoulder failed again a few weeks later, he had a new career opening up before him. In part, because of a meeting with Pauline and Don Edwards, which was about to happen.

Sylvie Reminisces

While Baz was checking the inside of his eyelids, Sylvie's thoughts went back to the early days of her and Barry's romance.

The difficult bit, she recalled, was the first three months. She was taken by this big, strong man. She was amazed at the way he had picked up the building and use of computers, but there was one other love in her life. The family time at their chalet at the Eden Gardens Sun Club. How would she cope if she had to give it all up for love?

Easter was only a few weeks away, normally the first time the family went to open the chalet for the summer. This was going to be a testing time for her new relationship.

She spoke to her parents about inviting Barry to join them at the club. Both her parents were keen to meet him. After all, he had made their daughter very happy, and it looked like he had given Dave a hand too. Dad suggested that it would be a good idea. Easter was late that year, but it was a Bank Holiday weekend and likely to rain. If it rained, there wouldn't be much by way of naked activity, so it would be a gentle introduction. If it didn't rain, well they would take it as it came.

That evening, she told Barry that on Easter Saturday her family would all be going to their summer place to get it ready for the summer. They would all like him to join them for lunch. The plan would be for him to pick her up mid-morning and drive her to the summer place.

Barry was back working, although his shoulder still hurt by the end of the day. On Good Friday, she had gone round to Barry's house. He was in a lot of pain she gave his shoulder a massage moving the muscles and tendons and allowing them to stretch and go back, relaxed. Barry's parents and sister came back from a family visit in the evening with bags of chips, fish pieces and sausages and the five of them ate and drank tea in front of the TV.

The next morning, Sylvie was nervous; she couldn't sit still. She paced back and forth between the lounge and the kitchen. She fidgeted with the radio. She washed up. She moved the chairs and changed her clothes twice. Surprisingly, the sun was shining and the day was warming up. Barry arrived bang on schedule. She ran out to the car and jumped into the passenger seat. They kissed.

"God, I'm nervous about meeting your folks," Barry looked really good in his smart trousers and a new shirt under his leather jacket.

"My parents aren't going to be your only problem, I'm sure about that," Sylvie was still on edge.

As Barry followed Sylvie's directions, he asked about their summer place. She told him, it was just a small chalet in a park, which had once been part of a stately home. She explained that her mum and dad had bought the place for the family when dad retired and mum had come into a little money when her parents passed.

They were still chatting when they pulled up at the gate to the club. Sylvie waved to the man on the gate. He recognised her and opened the gate. "Hi Stu," she called, as they drove through into the club grounds.

"I was worried something was up," he called back, "Your Mum and Dad got here hours ago, Dave and his lady friend got here half an hour before you too."

"Thanks, Stu," she replied. "Down there on the left, the car parking is just beyond the chalets." She instructed Barry, a nervous look on her face.

The park was still quiet; Sylvia pointed out the family chalet as they drove past it. Barry stopped the car where Sylvia indicated. Then they got out and Sylvie took Barry firmly by the hand and walked him back to the chalet.

"Sylvie! Yoo Hoo!" A voice called out. They both turned in the direction of the voice. Sylvie felt her heart sink as she saw Sassy waving; not that she had a problem with Sassy. Quite the opposite, she and Sassy were good mates. It was just she wanted to get Barry into the chalet before the issue of naturism came up. No chance of that now though Sassy was naked!

"Hi Sassy," she called back. "I have to dash; I'll catch up with you in a bit. Have fun!" She hurried the wide-mouthed Barry into the chalet.

Inside the chalet, Barry was introduced to Mr and Mrs Edwards, Pauline and Don. He said, "Hi", to Dave and shook hands with Sue, Dave's girlfriend.

Mr Edwards said, "Please call me Don," offered Barry a beer, and took him outside for a chat. Sylvie sat down close to the window so she could eavesdrop, her mum brought her a cup of tea and they listened together.

The two men sat and took a sip of their beer. Sylvie was pleased to hear Barry open the conversation.

"OK, where am I? I lost my bearings on the way here," Barry asked.

"Funny you should say baring," Don smiled "This is Eden Gardens Sun Club, it is a naturist club. The whole family are members here. This is where we come to relax over the summer."

"You mean that you all come here and take your clothes off and parade around naked in front of each other? Like Sassy was when we got here?"

Don explained that the word 'parade' was not really the right word. People just got on with doing whatever they would be doing at a holiday camp but without clothes. Always providing the weather was good enough of course!

Then the conversation moved on to work and life in general. Don was impressed with the way Barry had picked up the innovative use of small computers. He worked for a large company that used a large mainframe computer, which staff accessed from

110

terminals. This system was struggling; sometimes he had to wait hours for 'computer time to run important jobs. He could see a time when everybody would have an individual computer, like the ones Barry was building and teaching people to use. This was going to be the future.

"Lunch in five minutes," Pauline called. "Come and get washed up."

As they stood up, Barry picked up the beer cans. "Don, I was expecting you to ask me more about what my plans were towards Sylvia?"

"I just want the best for her. If you make the right choices and listen to good advice, you'll do the right thing, I'm sure. I think you are showing the right instincts by getting into this personal computing stuff." Don put a hand on his shoulder, "Let's go eat."

Sylvie took him to the bathroom so he could wash his hands. As she did, she gave him a quick kiss. "That went OK, didn't it?" Barry nodded, gave her a quick squeeze and went to wash his hands.

Lunch was a noisy affair as the family ate, laughed and talked. At the end of the meal, Don, Dave and Sue announced they were going to the clubhouse. Sylvie, Pauline and Barry were going to join them after the washing up. Sylvie had observed

Barry half-watching and trying not to watch as the three undressed and picked up towels, before leaving for the clubhouse.

This next half hour was going to be 'make or break' for her relationship with Barry.

They finished the drying up and put it all away in the compact kitchen's cupboards and cubbyholes. Pauline slipped off her clothes, picked up her towel, and with, "I'll order a pint and a half bitter for you two, see you soon!" She was gone.

Sylvie remembered the hug she gave the nervous Barry as if it was yesterday. She could feel him trembling in her arms. She had planned the next step. It was important to give Barry some control over what happened next. To give him some room to make his own choice about how the day ended.

"I'm going to the loo; I'll be right back," she had slipped out of his arms before he could react. In the bathroom, she quickly undressed, folding her clothes neatly. She wrapped a large towel around her and walked back into the living room. She walked up to the still bemused Barry and hugged him to her nearly naked body. "I'm going to sit outside with the paper when you are ready, come out and we'll go for that drink, or I'll walk you to the car." She had picked up the newspaper from the sofa and went outside.

She had only just finished the front page when Barry came out of the door. "What is this towel for?" he asked.

At that moment both their lives had changed forever and as far as Sylvie was concerned it was a change for the better.

Now her daughter had brought her own man to the same place, and he had bared all for the first time. Just like her Barry that Easter Saturday, too many years ago.

☐

The Councillor Bares Her Soul

In the clubhouse, Elaine and Brian were just ordering. "What would you both like?" Brian called over as they came through the patio doors.

"Can I have a coke please, Brian?"

"Make that two!"

Rags introduced Bea to Elaine and Brian and thanked them for the drinks.

"We wanted to thank you for the sensitive way you handled this, Rags," said Brian. "You could have caused Elaine and the whole family a lot of unpleasantness if you had gone about things another way."

"We weren't expecting you to be here today. We'd had this big idea, and we weren't sure about how to play things when we first saw you. We had assumed you weren't a naturist," he continued, "Then when we realised you were 'out of uniform' so to speak, we decided to take the risk and go ahead with our big gesture."

"What made you think I wasn't a naturist?" asked Rags.

"Silly man!" Bea giggled, "You didn't recognise the logo on the polo shirts. 'La Jenny' is a large naturist resort near Bordeaux! That you didn't know it by reputation marked you as a textile."

Turning to the other couple, "As far as I am aware, today is Rags' first experience of social nudity."

"Textile?" asked Rags, "I know … Later!"

"You handled it very well," said Elaine appreciatively.

"I am still a little confused, I had noticed that you weren't cotton-tailed and now I know why not. So how come Sean and Gill told me they only knew you through your council work?"

Brian and Elaine recounted their tale between them, while Rags and Bea listened over another round of drinks, captivated by the story.

Brian and Elaine had met at University, and at the end of their third year, after finals, they had, like hundreds of others, gone on a trip overland to Greece with another couple. They hadn't reached Greece, stopping in Yugoslavia. Here they found beaches along the Dalmatian Coast where people, mainly Germans swam and lay in the sun, naked. They rapidly settled into this naturist nirvana, living cheaply and naked for days on end. On their way back to the UK, the couple they were travelling with imploded. Sadly, they never heard from either of their travelling companions again. For the next few years, they returned to Yugoslavia, until they discovered France for Naturism. After that, they switched to the Atlantic coastal resorts. From the beaches of France, they watched with horror the ugly civil war that tore their former holiday destination apart. The two boys came along, but they continued to go to the naturist beaches of Europe as a family. Elaine's political career was now a real consideration, so they only went naked abroad. Then, as the children got older and started to notice that the other boys at school were cotton-tailed and the other boys noticed that they weren't, things had to change. They had given up their naturist holidays and gone to Portugal, Majorca, Disney Land and other family destinations.

It was the memories of these, early happy times that had made Elaine take up the case for Eden Gardens when Sean had asked for help.

Once re-awakened, those memories of their youthful, naked, carefree days in Yugoslavia and France washed over them at odd times. Leaving them feeling wistful. Then an email newsletter arrived, one that neither Elaine nor Brian remembered signing up to. It contained a special offer for an early-season break at La Jenny. Now the kids were older, maybe soon to fly the nest, they had gone for it. They had loved the experience.

While they were away, they had a long and soul-searching conversation about the rest of their lives. They had decided that they were going to make living clothes-free, when appropriate, part of their lives again. They had also decided that they were going to become part of naturism at home and join a club. Probably a club somewhere out of the immediate area, but in the UK, so they could enjoy time relaxing together in a clothes-free environment. PC Adiscombe's arrival on the doorstep had caused a rethink.

Elaine had spent her political life asking people she didn't know to trust her to act in their best interest. It was about time she demonstrated trust in some of her constituents too. So, they had changed their plans. The naked cuddle with their children was the first manifestation of the new plans. Their conversation with Sean and Gill over lunch had resulted in their membership application for Eden Gardens being passed immediately. They had joined the local club as part of their commitment to the concept of 'local'. They would be bringing the boys to the resort for the next few Sundays so that they could do litter collection as restitution for the damage they had done.

The youngsters were captivated by the tale and they had imagined themselves as the younger Brian and Elaine.

As the conversation tapered off Sean tapped Rags on the shoulder.

"There is someone I think you should meet, my Forensic Expert. Before you do, are you going to become a member here?"

"I have had a great day today; I have made some good friends here too." He squeezed Bea's hand, "A lot of your members will know who I am after my 'naming' today and the rest will have seen me running around bare. I'll do the paperwork tomorrow if I may?"

"Super, I saw you enjoying the pool and of course, you and Bea make a great couple. Welcome to the club! Now come along with me," Sean continued, "We will go and find my expert."

As they walked towards the other end of the bar, Rags recognised one woman from the boy's illicit photographs. She was talking to a second woman, who had her back to them.

Sean called to her, "Jane, I just wanted to introduce Rags. Although I think you two might have already met?"

As Jane turned, Rags started as he recognised Jane Deene, the SOCO. No wonder Sean had wanted the camera analysed by her! They exchanged greetings and both expressed surprise at finding someone from work here. Then shaking hands in as if to seal a deal of mutual confidentiality, they parted.

Rags went to find Bea. He found her talking to her parents. Barry and Sylvie were going over to a friend's chalet for a drink or two and they were staying at the resort overnight. Bea announced that she and Rags were going to the cinema and then having a meal, she'd probably stay at his place tonight.

Rags kept his mouth shut.

They went over the way to Grandma's Summer Place, dressed and walked to Rags' car hand in hand. Less than an hour later, they were making great movies of their own and feasting on each other. The cinema and meal out were never really going to happen!

*****

Late the next morning, Sylvie found Rags and Bea side by side at the pool.

"Dad has gone to work," she informed the couple, "and I have to go in to work after lunch, I'm on a late today. So, you are on your own."

Then she addressed Rags directly, "Make sure she gets on with her revision, her exam is less than two weeks off."

"Mother!"

"I'd hate for you to fail this late in the day, Honey. Rags please make sure she works!"

"I'm back on duty tomorrow, but I'll make sure she gets started today," Rags reassured her.

Sylvie went off to dress for work. Rags reached out and held his lover's hand.

120

"Give your Mum an hour and we will go back to the chalet and you can tell me all about Contract and Tort, while I give you a massage. Meanwhile, let's finish this membership application form, I didn't realise that being a single male would make it so difficult. I know they have to weed out undesirables but this..."

"It isn't just the undesirables, there is a problem with the balance of the sexes and there are the rights of the LBGT community to consider too," interrupted Bea.

"Sounds like you are back at work already. Give me a kiss and let's go and have a swim before you get stuck into your books."

With that, the uncovered policeman and naked solicitor stood up, held hands and walked together across the grass, where two naked teenage boys were picking up litter, and passed the miniten courts.

"Next week," said Bea "I'll explain next week!"

The End – For Now.

- -

Thank you for reading the Uncovered Policeman.

I hope you enjoyed it.

To whet your appetite here is the first chapter of the second story in the series!

The Uncovered Policeman Abroad

Keeping Mum

PC Adiscombe, Addy to his friends and colleagues in the force, also known as Rags to his friends outside of work, was due a couple of days off. The weather forecast for the coming week was typical British summer weather: cloud, rain, some sunshine and little prospect of snow. He was sitting with his new girlfriend of just a couple of months trying to sort out what to do with the time. Bea was waiting for the results of her final Licence to Practice Course exams. She was well on the way to becoming a solicitor. "Shame about the weather or we could have had a break at Grandma's Summer Place." This was the name by which Bea and her family referred to the chalet they owned at Eden Gardens Naturist Resort. Both PC Adiscombe and Bea were members at Eden Gardens. It was where they had met earlier that summer and where Bea and the other naturists had given him the name of Rags.

Bea's family were long-time multigenerational naturists. Bea's decision to go to university, the first person in the family to do so, had been a cause for celebration. That she was now on the verge of becoming a solicitor was seen as the best thing the family had ever achieved. It didn't count that her mum, Sylvia, was a Ward Manager in the local hospital, that Barry, her father, ran his own IT consultancy business, or that her elder brother had graduated from Sandhurst and recently been promoted to Captain. Her younger brother was in his final year before graduating as a Physiotherapist. Her baby sister was trying for medical school. Still, with all that success Bea was going to be the first lawyer in the family. She loved her family but found being the star a bit trying. Her great loves in life were Rags, laughing at the absurdities of life and the feel of the sun on her skin.

When she and Rags were relaxing at Grandma's Summer Place so often she had all three at once. Plus, now that her exams were over and the results were in the future Bea was in a very happy place.

As she came around from her reverie she caught Rags reluctantly sighing. "I suppose I should go and see my Mum. I haven't seen her for months."

"How about I come along too, would that make it easier to cope with?" suggested Bea.

Bea had an ulterior motive for wanting to meet Rags' mother but she wasn't going to remind him.

Rags noticed that her eyes, or more specifically the golden flecks in her chocolate brown eyes, were dancing. He had first noticed her dancing eyes the day they met. He knew that this was a certain sign Bea was happy and this always made him happy too. That was it.

On Sunday morning, they were up at the crack of late breakfast and on the road. Just before lunchtime, they pulled up outside the small semi on a 1950s estate that Rags had called home for twelve of the previous twenty-four years. He climbed out of the car and collected the bottle of wine from the back seat. Moving round to the passenger side he took the bunch of flowers from Bea then shut and locked the door after she got out of the car.

They were met at the door by a well-dressed woman in her early fifties. The official description would have included she was just short of average height and just over average weight but would not have included the fact that for her age, she was a 'cracker', a fact that the man in her life constantly reminded her of. After greeting them both and graciously accepting both the gifts she took them through to the living room.

"Jeremy not here?" enquired Rags of his defacto stepfather of 5 years.

"No, he has gone to the cricket. He said it would be easier for Bea if she met us one at a time. I think he just wanted to watch the Aussies being slaughtered from the stands rather than on the TV."

"Sit down Bea; I'm Rosie by the way; I know Sabbath doesn't like using real names. Would you like a glass of wine before lunch? I know Sabbath will have a beer."

Bea managed a stifled "Yes please, a red if possible," to Rosie as the hostess went through to the kitchen.

Bea's eyes danced as she bit on a knuckle trying to suppress her almost hysterical laughter.

The dancing eyes and the playful smile were, as far as Rags was concerned, number one on his list of the '25 Best Things About Bea'. Seeing the golden flecks in her chocolate brown eyes dance as the corners of her mouth twitched from laughter to smile and back again almost countered his embarrassment. Then he remembered the conversation back in early June before he became Rags, in which he had told Bea she would never discover his given name from anybody except his Mum. This made him glow inside;

128

they were still on life's journey together and still laughing.

Three hours later Bea and Rosie were chatting over the washing up like lifelong friends. Together they took a tray of coffee and some biscuits through to the sun lounge where Addy was looking through the absent Jeremy's newspaper.

Handing him a cup of black coffee Bea asked, "would you like a biscuit with that Rags?"

"Rags? That is a new one on me," interjected Rosie. "Most of his friends call him Addy. He won't use his real name. He says it is embarrassing."

"Well," Bea replied mischievously, "I'm not sure I should tell you this."

"Oh No!" thought Rags, "more embarrassment. How much can I take in one day?"

"Has he told you much about how we met?"

Rosie shook her head.

"Well, I am a member of a recreation club. Earlier in the year, we had a break-in and this hunk was sent to investigate. I was rather captivated by his shy retiring manner so I arranged for us to bump into each other as often as possible. By the end, we had hit it off so well he decided that he would join the club too."

"Nicely played, but why Rags?" encouraged Rosie as Rags hid himself away behind the financial pages.

"I suppose it is because the nature of the club is not what you'd call mainline. Everyone uses first names or nicknames to avoid revealing other people's identity in public by accident, and there was no way I was going around with an Addy," Bea explained.

"You don't do historical re-enactments, Sealed Knot or Vikings or something like that? Please tell me you don't," pleaded Rosie

"No, not quite that far off centre; we are naturists." Bea finished in a matter-of-fact manner.

"Is that all? Well, that is a relief, I had visions of you wenching while he did pike drill or whatever." Raising her voice to Rags: "Your father and I talked about visiting a nudist club many times, but we felt we couldn't while you and your brother were at school. That is why we had this room built so we could sit out with the doors open on nice days and enjoy the sun."

"So that is why the front door was always locked and I wasn't allowed a key until I was 14!" exclaimed Rags, as he lowered the paper.

"Come on then Bea, we are past that block. Why is my son called Rags?"

"Well," Bea continued conspiratorially, "until the first time he joined us in the pool he was PCCP, PC Cutie Pants. I knew that couldn't last, but as I said I am not the sort of girl to go out with an Addy. Then on the day of his first venture into naturism, we all noticed his tan stopped where his trunks had been. In naturist parlance, he was a cotton-tail, having a white behind like the cotton-tailed rabbit. From there I remembered my Dad's Christmas present, an old BBC Watch With Mother DVD, I got the title wrong I thought it was ...."

"Rag Tag and Bobtail from Tales of the Riverbank ... not the rabbit but the rabbit's friend!" interrupted Rosie. "How clever and quick of you! I might call him that too if I may, seeing as he hates Sabbath."

*****

"I like your Mum." Rags was driving home, Bea had emerged from a thoughtful silence. "But Sabbath, that must have been tough. Did the other kids call you Black or Ozzy?"

"Neither," grunted Rags as he changed gear and accelerated away past a slower car.

"Why Sabbath anyway? Our birthdays are on the same day of the week; I'm a year younger and I'm a Thursday child so you must have been born on a Wednesday."

Rags slowed the car back to just under the limit.

"OK, time for the whole story," he sighed. "Just don't laugh too loudly or I'll make you walk home."

He pulled off the main road, drove a few hundred yards down a quiet lane, pulled into a field gateway and stopped the engine.

"I wish they had called me Ozzy or Black in my secondary school. It was much worse." He paused. "I am named Sabbath because I was conceived one Sunday Afternoon, during a post-lunch laydown."

Bea giggled.

"They gave me a middle name; the town they were visiting that weekend. Faversham after the town

132

in Kent. So being a bloke I couldn't use that without the lads all wanting to know how I got that name."

The golden flecks in Bea's eyes were in motion as she struggled to stop herself from laughing out loud.

"Then Mum went and capped it all. She had name tags made up for me and my brother for our school uniforms. To save money she had the one set of tags made up. Three initials and our surname. He got the Adiscombe half of the labels. I got the initials. All my kit was labelled SFA … yeah, I was 'Sweet Fuck All' for two years, until they opened a new school. I transferred to the new school as Addy Adiscombe"

If it hadn't been for the seat belt, Bea would have been writhing on the floor. Regaining control, she put her arms around him, kissed him and held him. Because while she had a wicked sense of humour she was a kind girl and she loved her man. Besides, biting his jacket stopped her laughing even more.

An hour later they were back on the road.

"So," said Bea in the temporary lull now her giggles had stopped. "What is your brother's name?"

A smiling Rags told her it was his secret to tell. "Unless Mum blows that secret too," he added, and they both laughed the rest of the way back to Rags' flat.

Let the next adventure begin!

OTHER BOOKS BY TED BUN

Rags to Riches Novellas

The Uncovered Policeman
The Uncovered Policeman Abroad
The Uncovered Policeman: In and Out of the Blues
The Uncovered Policeman: Goodbye Blues
Two Weddings and a Naming
The Uncovered Policeman: Caribbean Blues
The Uncovered Policeman: Family Album
A Spring Break at L'Abeille Nue
The Uncovered Policeman: Made for TV
The Uncovered Policeman: The Long Road
The Uncovered Policeman: Live, Laugh and Love
The Uncovered Policeman: A New Home in the Sun
While Bees Sleep

Rags to Riches Short Stories

The Cutters' Tale
The Naked Warriors
The Girls Trip to the Beach
Cocoa and Pyjamas
Forty Shades of Green
BareAid

The Uncovered Policeman's Casebooks

Other Novellas

New House … New Neighbours
New House … New Address
New House … New Traditions

The Summer of '71 (A Crooke and Loch story)
Runners and Riders (A Crooke and Loch story)
The Summer of '76 (A Crooke and Loch story)

Problems and Passions (NBL Solutions 1)
Problems of Succession (NBL Solutions 2)
Problems in the Pyrenees (NBL Solutions 3)

The Day Before Last

When the Music Stops: DC al Fine
Then Play On

The Girl with a Ginger Cat

Other Short Stories
Going South – Forever
The Dancer
A Job in the City
Blindman, Buff
Flat Bares

Meet Ted Bun

 I was born in London in 1956 and have lived most of my life in the South of England.

Ted Bun came into existence in 2005 with the launch of the website 'The Sun On Our Buns' (www.sunnybuns.me.uk). The pseudo name was necessary because I was working for a large national organisation and association with naturism would not have gone down well!

Strangely, although I know nothing about how computers work my work at that time was largely to do with IT projects. I suppose what I was doing was process redesign. Then we were reorganised and suddenly I found myself working as an independent contractor.

A few years later and independent contractors were all on the way out.

Looking in H&E Naturist one month, I saw an article/advert for a small naturist resort in Portugal that was available for rental. The ideal opportunity for Ted Bun to start his new career!

Three fun-filled summers later, Mrs Bun decided this was what we wanted to do. We then spent two years searching for the right house to leave the rat race behind. Then we found L'Olivette, our little piece of paradise in South West France, and we have started offering relaxing holidays by sharing our gîte and our lives with people who love nature, see it at www.handluggageholidays.co.uk

During the long evenings of the quieter season, here in L'Olivette, a series of novellas and short stories started to take shape, The Rags to Riches series.

This, my first book in which our central characters first meet, and romance starts. 'The Uncovered Policeman', was first published on Valentine's Day 2016.

You can e-mail me at- ted.bun@sunnybuns.me.uk

Or follow my blog at www.tvhost.co.uk

138

Or why not come and share our little bit of paradise sometime?

Printed in Great Britain
by Amazon